26.8.23

KT-558-030

Honeypie

Petalbright

Sparkletail

Candyheart

Sugarwing

Snufflesnort

Starshine

Twinkletoes

Lavender

Lollipop

For Sammy
with the day-glo nails – M.S.

To baby Rosie,
sweet dreams xx – T.B.

Published in the UK by Scholastic, 2021
Euston House, 24 Eversholt Street, London, NW1 1DB
Scholastic Ireland, 89E Lagan Road, Dublin Industrial Estate, Glasnevin, Dublin, D11 HP5F

SCHOLASTIC and associated logos are trademarks and/or
registered trademarks of Scholastic Inc.

Text © Mark Sperring, 2021
Illustrations © Tim Budgen, 2021

The rights of Mark Sperring and Tim Budgen to be identified
as the author and illustrator of this work have been asserted
by them under the Copyright, Designs and Patents Act 1988.

ISBN 978 0702 30695 2

A CIP catalogue record for this book is available from the British Library.

Printed in China
Paper made from wood grown in sustainable forests and other controlled sources.

1 3 5 7 9 10 8 6 4 2

www.scholastic.co.uk

MARK SPERRING

TIM BUDGEN

20 UNICORNS at BEDTIME

SCHOLASTIC

Once upon a twinkling night,
Mindy could NOT sleep.

So, her daddy and her
favourite toy said . . .

"You should count
some sheep!"

Now, Mindy isn't keen on sheep,
they "BAAAAAAA" from dusk till dawn.

So, instead of counting
noisy sheep,
she counted . . .

Unicorns!

1...

Here's a unicorn
kicking its hooves high.

2...

Here's a unicorn beneath a rainbow'd sky!

3...

Here's a unicorn
munching on some hay.

4...

Here's a unicorn who danced about all day!

5...

Here's a unicorn with daisies round its neck.

7...

Here's a unicorn who watched
the daylight fade.

8...

Here's a unicorn who
found a moonlit glade.

9...
Here's a unicorn
lulled by a lullaby.

10...
Here's a unicorn who
gave a gentle sigh.

11...
Here's a unicorn by a sleepy stream.

12...
Here's a unicorn who's whispering, "Sweet dreams."

Yes, once upon a twinkling night,
while counting unicorns,

Mindy gave her toy a hug,
and then, a great, big yawn.

But, in her dreams, she kept on counting fine four-legged chums.

13...

14...

15...

And, there's still
more yet to come!

16...

Here's a unicorn with tangles in its mane.

18...

Here's a unicorn beneath the bright starlight.

19...

Here's a unicorn who needs a kiss goodnight!

20!

Here's a unicorn who
flew down from on high,

Mindy climbed
upon its back . . .

then, closed
her sleepy eyes . . .

They flew up to this castle
where they both snuggly lay.

Once upon a twinkling night,
'till daybreak broke next day.